For Xianne and Xzjuan.
Being your mom is
my greatest blessing.
Dare to live boldly, be brave,
and always remember that
you are enough just by being you.
I LOVE YOU.
                                    -Mom

Library of Congress Control Number::2021914734

Help promote inclusion. Purchase two and donate to your local audiologist clinic and local elementary school.

www.princesslizziebooks.com

Princess Lizzie

Learns Manners

Written by: Tosombra Kimes

Illustrated by: Karla Bivens

Princess Lizzie is five years old.

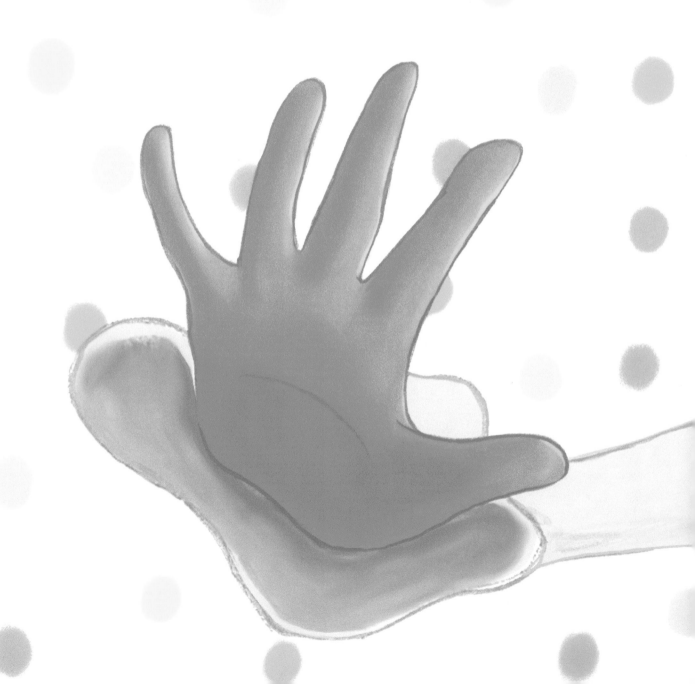

She knows she must do just what she's told.

When her mom says, "Clean your room."

Princess Lizzie asks for help
to use the vacuum.

When her dad says, "It's time for bed."
She closes her eyes
and does just what he says.

No talking back.

No yelling.

No crying.
No kicking,

Or stomping her feet.

No ignoring her parents
whenever they speak.

Princess Lizzie knows
how to earn her crown.

Listen to her parents so they will smile and not frown.

So now you, too, can do
what Princess Lizzie would do.

Because every child with manners
is a prince or princess, too.

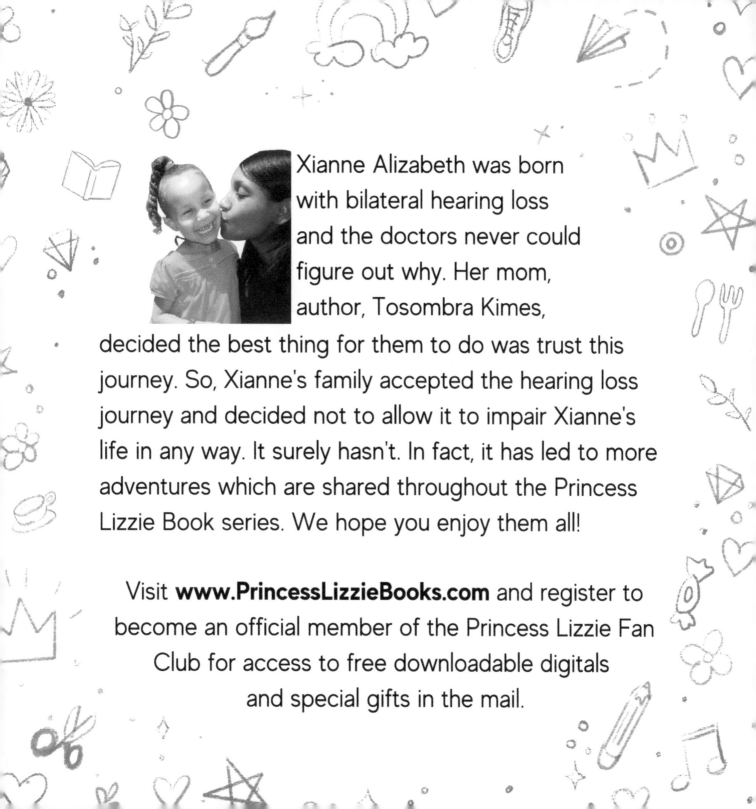

Xianne Alizabeth was born with bilateral hearing loss and the doctors never could figure out why. Her mom, author, Tosombra Kimes, decided the best thing for them to do was trust this journey. So, Xianne's family accepted the hearing loss journey and decided not to allow it to impair Xianne's life in any way. It surely hasn't. In fact, it has led to more adventures which are shared throughout the Princess Lizzie Book series. We hope you enjoy them all!

Visit **www.PrincessLizzieBooks.com** and register to become an official member of the Princess Lizzie Fan Club for access to free downloadable digitals and special gifts in the mail.